Glenwood

JUL
AUG

S0-ACM-536

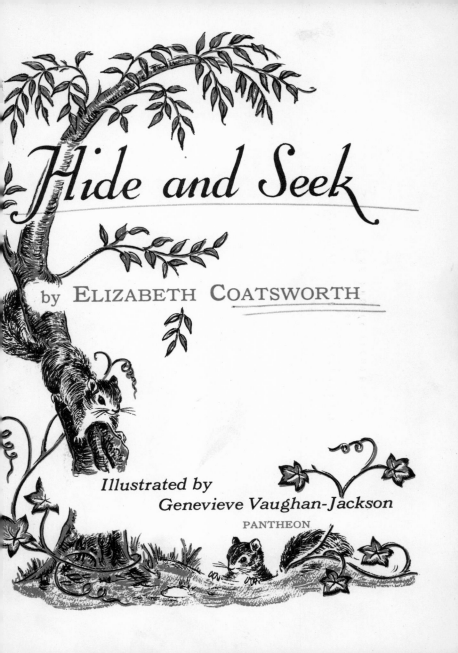

Hide and Seek

by ELIZABETH COATSWORTH

Illustrated by
Genevieve Vaughan-Jackson

PANTHEON

For

Jean and Cathy

with much love

HIDE AND SEEK

Where are you?

Underground?

Like a prairie dog or mole,

or a woodchuck in its hole?

Or a rabbit

or a fox

in a den among the rocks?

There's no sound.
Have you gone
underground?

Where are you?

Are you there
in a cave with a bear
sleeping winter through?

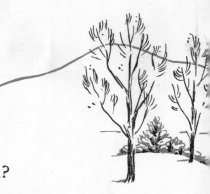

Are you in some hollow tree
with a squirrel
or a bee?

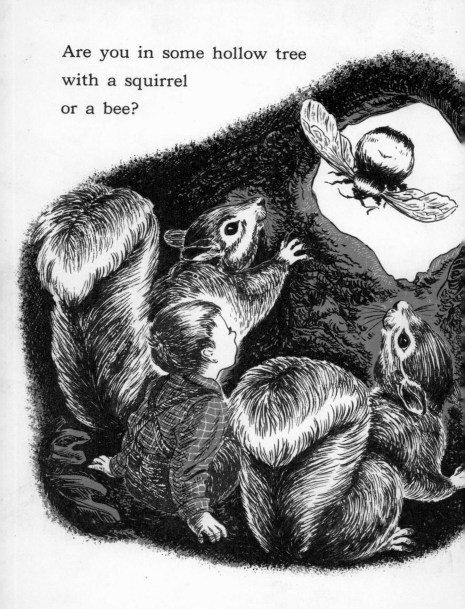

Where are you?

Where are you?

In a nest
with blue eggs
beneath the breast
of a robin
or a thrush?

Are you in some flowering bush
with a goldfinch
or song sparrow
where I cannot, cannot
follow?
    Where are you?

Where are you?

In some cocoon

waking butterflies up too soon?

Or a moth

with dusty wings?

Are you in the silver cone
of the wasps?
Or all alone
under bark
in the dark?

Where are you?

Where are you?

In the hay
of the manger
hid away?

Does the cow know

or old Ben?

Do the sheep guess,

or the hen,

or the duck?

Are you hidden in the truck

or the car?

Who will tell me where you are?

Where are you?

In the house,

walled up safe with rat or mouse?

High up in a spider's web
gossiping with some old spider,
sitting cozily beside her?

Or with crickets
on the hearth,
playing on a fiddle, too?

Where are you?

Where are you?

On a train?
Charging over hill and plain,
hooting, tooting at the crossways,
puffing, luffing at the stations,
sliding, gliding down the tracks,
while the houses turn their backs?

Rain or shine,
shine or rain,
are you travelling on the train?

If you aren't on any train,
have you flown off in a plane,
high, high,
     in the sky,
seeing earthly girls and boys
smaller than the smallest toys,
thimble houses, tea-cup town,
fields like stamps, some green, some brown,

Finger ridges,
    match-sized bridges—
flying higher than a swallow,
hawk or eagle ever flew—
    Where are you?

Whencesoever,
come back soon
from your cave
or from your bough

From your burrow or cocoon,
or your shelter in the barn,
from the quick and thundering train,
from the soaring, roaring plane,
from the zenith of the sky—

COME

HOME

1568 SOON!